THIS BOOK BELONGS TO

_____

The Adventures of
Bella & Harry
Let's Visit Dublin!

Written By
Lisa Manzione

Illustrated By
Kristine Lucco

Bella & Harry, LLC

www.BellaAndHarry.com
email: BellaAndHarryGo@aol.com

"**Bella**, be sure to bring some extra pennies for our next family vacation!"

"Why, Harry?"

5

"We are off to Dublin, Ireland with our family.
We will need extra pennies to cross the Ha'penny Bridge!"

"**Harry**, you don't need pennies to cross the first iron bridge in Ireland anymore. Opened in 1816, the Ha'penny Bridge (also known as the Wellington Bridge and the Liffey Bridge) was built to replace the seven ferries, or boats, that took people back and forth across the Liffey River. In the beginning there was a charge (or fee) to cross the bridge. After 1919 there was no longer a fee to cross the bridge."

"Okay Bella, I won't bring any extra pennies."

"**Hey**, do you think we will meet any leprechauns in Dublin, Ireland?"

8

"**NO** Harry. We will not meet
any leprechauns, but we will see a lot
of great sights such as Trinity College Library, Giant's Causeway,
Blarney Castle and the Cliffs of Moher."

"**Bella**, are you sure we won't meet any leprechauns?
I would really like to meet a leprechaun and make a wish!"

"No Harry. Leprechauns are mythical creatures from stories, and don't really exist."

"Hmmm..."

10

"Let's go! We are boarding our flight to the 'Emerald Isle'."

"Bella, I thought we were going to Dublin, Ireland."

Atlantic Ocean

SCOTLAND

NORTHERN IRELAND

IRELAND

Irish Sea

DUBLIN

WALES

ENGLAND

"Harry, Ireland is sometimes called the 'Emerald Isle' because of the beautiful green colors of the grass, hills and mountains. Ireland gets a lot of rain due to its location on earth. Let's check our map while we are on our flight. Dublin, Ireland is here. Ireland is the third largest island in Europe."

"Come on Harry, our first stop in Dublin is Trinity College. Trinity College has the largest library in Ireland. The 'Old Library' building at Trinity College holds one of the most important books in history. It is called 'The Book of Kells'. 'The Book of Kells' is considered one of Ireland's best treasures."

"**Bella**, what makes this book so special?"

"**Let's** go Harry! We are heading to Giant's Causeway which is about three hours away."

"**Giants!** Bella, do you think we will see the famous Irish giant Finn McCool? Legend says that Finn created the causeway, or steps, because he was mad at the giant in Scotland!"

"**No** Harry, the story about Finn McCool is just a myth.
Giant's Causeway is an area of stones (interlocking basalt columns).
It is believed the causeway was formed by a volcano a very long time ago."

"So, we aren't going to see any giants while we are visiting Ireland?"

"No Harry. We are not going to see any giants."

"What about fairies? Do you think we will see any fairies while we are in Ireland?"

"Oh Harry, no. We will not see any leprechauns, giants or fairies
while we are in Ireland."

"**Look!** Our family is taking a walk on the rocks. Let's go with them!"

"Bella, this is fun! I have never walked on rocks made by a volcano before!"

"**Our** next stop on our tour is Blarney Castle.
I can't wait to kiss the Blarney Stone!"

"Bella, why do you want to kiss a stone?"

"**Well**, Ireland is full of legends and myths. It is said that if you kiss the Blarney Stone, you will have the 'gift of gab' forever. That means you will speak easily to others Harry.

It is not easy to get to the stone. We have to walk to the top of the castle, then hang upside down over the edge of the castle to kiss the stone! So, let's go!"

"WOW, Bella! What a pretty castle!"

"Yes Harry, the castle has been here for about 600 years. This is the third castle that has been built on this spot. The first castle was built of wood. It was torn down and replaced by a stone castle. The second castle was torn down and today we are in the third Blarney Castle which is also made of stone."

"Okay Harry, it is my turn to kiss the Blarney Stone! Hold my paws so I don't fall.

Yay! I kissed the stone! I will have the 'gift of gab' forever!"

"Oh, great!"

23

"It is time for lunch Harry. We are heading to Cork City, Ireland for an Irish meal.

Today we are having Irish stew made of lamb, potatoes and onions, along with Irish soda bread. The bread is not sweet but it is very tasty. The bread has a crunchy crust, and is soft on the inside. For dessert we are having chocolate potato cake and apple barley pudding!"

"**Next** stop...the Cliffs of Moher! The cliffs are 702 feet above sea level. Many people believe this is one of the most beautiful sites in Ireland. Look, you can see the Aran Islands and Galway Bay. Harry? Harry?"

"Harry! Harry! What are you doing? Come back here!"

"**Bella**, I love chasing birds!"

"Harry! STOP! You can't chase the birds! These birds are special cliff nesting seabirds, protected by Ireland."

"Whoa, Bella, what is that?"

28

"**Harry**, this is O'Brien's Tower. It is a good thing you stopped chasing the birds or you might have missed this tower!"

"Let's climb to the top of the tower!"

"Wow! We can see up and down the beautiful emerald green coastline of Ireland!"

"Bella, I heard there are no snakes in Ireland. Is that true?"

"Yes Harry. That is true. Thousands of years ago it got very cold in Ireland (a time in history called the Ice Age) and the snakes could not live here. You see Harry, snakes are cold-blooded animals and need very warm weather to live."

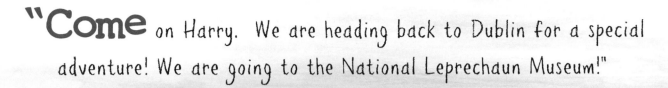

"**Come** on Harry. We are heading back to Dublin for a special adventure! We are going to the National Leprechaun Museum!"

"Yay! I knew there were leprechauns in Ireland!"

Well, Harry and I are at our final stop in Dublin with our family, the National Leprechaun Museum. We had a great time visiting Ireland! We hope you have too! For now it is slán, or good-bye, from Bella Boo and Harry too!

Our Adventure to Dublin

Bella and Harry with step dancers.

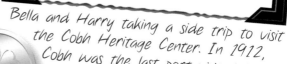

Bella and Harry taking a side trip to visit the Cobh Heritage Center. In 1912, Cobh was the last port visited by a ship named the "RMS Titanic."

Bella and Harry having fun with an Irish Wolfhound and other friends.

Bella and Harry crossing the Carrick-a-Rede Rope Bridge.

Fun Irish Gaelic Words and Phrases

Dia dhuit - Hello

Fáilte - Welcome

Maidin mhaith - Good morning

Oíche mhaith - Good night

Cailín - Girl

Madra - Dog

Go raibh maith agat - Thank you

Library of Congress Cataloging-in-Publications Data is available

Manzione, Lisa

The Adventures of Bella & Harry: Let's Visit Dublin!

ISBN: 978-1-937616-51-9

First Edition

Book Eleven of Bella & Harry Series

For further information please visit:

www.BellaAndHarry.com

or

Email: BellaAndHarryGo@aol.com

Printed in the United States of America

Lehigh Phoenix, Hagerstown, Maryland

October 2013

13 10 11 LP 1 1